TERRY DEARY'S
GREEK TALES

THE BOY WHO CRIED HORSE

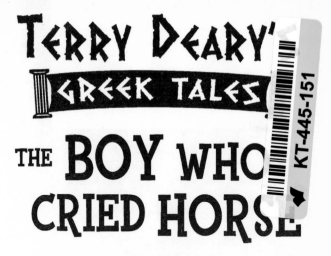

Illustrated by Helen Flook

A & C Black • London

First published 2007 by
A & C Black Publishers Ltd
38 Soho Square, London, W1D 3HB

www.acblack.com

Text copyright © 2007 Terry Deary
Illustrations copyright © 2007 Helen Flook

ISBN 0-7136-8216-7
ISBN 978-0-7136-8216-8

A CIP catalogue for this book is available from the British Library.

This book is produced using paper that is made from wood grown in
managed, sustainable forests. It is natural, renewable and recyclable.
The logging and manufacturing processes conform to the
environmental regulations of the country of origin.

Printed and bound in Great Britain by Bookmarque Ltd, Croydon.

Introduction

Troy, 1180 BC

Aesop the Greek storyteller said:
*There is no believing a liar, even
when he speaks the truth.*

I live in an invisible city. The city of Troy. Once, the finest city in the world. It's not there now. It's gone. The wind blows across the plains and covers the stones with sand and dust.

How can this be? you ask. How could a mighty city turn to a crumbling ruin in my lifetime?

I will tell you, if you will listen. Troy would still be there now if they had listened to me back then. The trouble was I told lies.

But I'm not lying now.

You believe me, don't you? I am Acheron the Liar. The last Trojan. And this is my story. Listen and learn...

Chapter One

My mother used to tell me stories.

"I'll not forget the day you were born," she'd say. "The day our brave Prince Paris came to Troy. He stood upon the palace steps and spoke."

Then Mother would stand and raise her chin. Her eyes would gaze into the distance and she became our prince. "People Trojan, greet you I with deep joy, godly thanks give us for journey safely homeward be today in shiply sail."

"Why does he speak like that?"
I'd ask.

Mother would shake her head.
"Our Paris is good with a sword.
Hopeless with words. He tangles
them up like wet washing on a
windy day."

And then she'd tell me how Prince Paris showed the Trojans his new wife, Queen Helen. "Lovelier than a great steak pie," she'd sigh.

When you are starving every day, then *nothing* is lovelier than a great steak pie. We were lucky to get a little rat meat in our watery soup.

The trouble was Prince Paris had *stolen* Queen Helen from the Greeks. And no sooner had he landed back in Troy, than the Greeks arrived...

"We want her back!" her husband, Menelaus, said. "We'll stay right here, outside your walls, until you starve to death."

"Not a chancely hopeful thing, think I," Prince Paris laughed. "We overstuffy with foodlets!"

"And that happened the day you were born," my mother said. "Ten hungry years later, and still we battle on."

In the palace, Prince Paris found ways to feed the people. Troy was a huge city with many little gates to sneak food in. A deep well in the market place made sure that we had water.

The best food went to Paris and Helen, and the next best to the fighting men who stood guard on Troy's massive walls.

The next best went to the people working in the palace. The rest of us were left to live on scraps – or any rats that we could catch.

But soon even the rats were as thin as the east wind that blew across the plains of Troy.

And that was why I learned to be a storyteller.

Every Friday, they had a feast at the palace. They ate proper pies with tender goat or dog meat and gorgeous greasy gravy. Poets sang stories of the heroes and were paid with a pie.

I learned to write poems and sing them to Paris and Helen. Long story poems that went on for half a feast.

Of course, the tales I told were lies. I made Paris and the Trojan heroes sound like gods because that's what they wanted to hear. I made the

Greeks appear as weak as the seaweed on the shores where their ships rested.

So I am a liar. If you were hungry, then you'd lie, too.

Chapter Two

That Friday evening was the last evening Troy would ever see. It was the evening I met the stranger. I met  him on the road to the palace. He was an old man with a grey beard and a dusty robe. He slipped from the shadow of a side street and stopped me.

He pointed at the tortoise shell I carried. "You have a lyre," he said. "You must be a poet."

"I am. I'm going to sing for Paris and Helen at the palace."

"Then I'll come along with you," he said. "You can show me the way."

"Everyone knows where the palace is," I said.

"I am a stranger," he told me.

I walked a few paces over the paved road, then stopped. "There are no strangers in Troy. The city has been locked for ten years to keep out the Greeks. How did you get in?"

"There are ways," he said softly. "Lead on. Perhaps you can help me get inside the palace. I need to speak to Paris."

"Why should I help you?"

"I'll give you all the food you ever dreamed of ... and more," he promised.

I said I'd lie to help him. If you were hungry then you'd lie, too. I didn't know I'd betray my city, did I?

We walked on through the moonlit streets to the palace. The wind from the plains seemed to shake the moon and pushed us up the hill. The guards knew me well and let me through. "Who's this?" they asked and pointed at the man.

"My dad," I lied. My dad had died fighting in the first few weeks of the war. I'd never known him. I always thought he'd be like this kind-eyed, grey-haired, old man.

The palace hall was bustling with servants and guards, magicians and jugglers, dancers and musicians. I knew them all.

Torches flamed and crackled along the walls. A trumpet blasted out a tuneless fanfare*.

"Ooops! Sorry – a few wrong notes in there!" the trumpeter grinned. "I proudly present my Lord Paris and his Lady Helen!"

* I'm a singer. I hate bad music. Sorry, but it has to be said: the trumpeter should have been shot with a poisoned arrow.

The people clapped politely and
Paris entered. He was followed by
the sly-eyed, sour-mouthed Helen.
(That's what my mother says now.)

Paris raised a hand. "Commencify
us the juggly and the musi-magic
singerly songerly entertainables!"

The stranger muttered in my ear,
"What is he saying?"

"Don't know," I shrugged. "It's all Greek to me."

We watched the dancers snake and sway, and a magician who made a duck appear from Helen's hat.

Then it was my turn. But as I stepped forward with my lyre,

the stranger pushed me aside. He bowed before Paris.

"Whattalie wantable?" Paris asked.

"News," the stranger said. "I bring great news!"

Chapter Three

"My name," the stranger said, "is Sinon, and I come from the Greek camp."

Helen jumped to her feet. "A Greek? In Troy? Kill him, guards! Kill him!"

There was a swish of swords as the guards marched forwards but Sinon raised a hand. "I hate the Greeks!" he cried. "They are cowards on the battlefield. Mighty Paris here is greater than *ten* Greek warriors!"

"It's truthly rightable," Paris said.

"What I came to tell you," Sinon went on, "is that the Greeks are running away."

"*Away?*" Helen said and her sly eyes squinted at the old man.

"Back to Greece. They say they have been here too long. That they have more important things to do. Other wars to fight. They have sailed off in their ships and left behind a mighty wooden statue to remember their heroes!"

"They *have* no heroes," Helen sneered.

"Not herolic like Paris princelet!" Paris laughed.

"Their statue will stand on the windy plain of Troy for all the world to see," Sinon said softly. "Every ship that passes will see it and remember the Greek heroes."

"*Statue?*" Helen asked. "What is this statue? A statue of some hated hero like Achilles?"

"Paris princelet arrowed Achilleres in the heel-o and deaded him dead with tippy point poison*!" Paris cried.

---

* That was true. Paris was too much of a coward to face the great Greek Achilles in battle. He shot him from behind with a poison arrow. Of course, I didn't sing *that* story in my poems!

"It is the statue of a horse," Sinon said. "You can see it from the city walls. Maybe it is a gift from the Greeks to noble Paris. It will stand there and remind you of them every day."

"No it won't!" Helen roared.
"It won't?" Sinon said.

"No. We will bring it into the city and use it for firewood. We will not let passing ships see anything Greek," she raged. "Paris ... give the order!"

"Ahem!" Paris cleared his throat. "Statute horsling insideify Troylum getter sunshiny day."

The guards stood still. "What did he say?" one asked.

Helen sighed and explained. "Tomorrow at first light we'll drag the wooden horse inside the city."

"That'll be hard work. We'll need lots of pies to give us strength," a guard grumbled.

"Now the Greeks have gone we'll never go hungry again. You'll have pies tonight and pies every day of your life!" Helen promised.

Of course she didn't know their "lives" from that night on would be short. Very short. Very, very short.

Chapter Four

The feast began before I could sing my new poem. I saw Sinon the stranger slip out of the palace hall, and I followed him. I would return and sing for my pie after the feast.

Sinon said he was a Greek who hated Greeks ... but he didn't say why. I didn't trust the man.

The stranger hurried back down the moonlit hill to the spot where he'd met me. He turned into a bat-black alley and headed for the north wall. I followed and watched.

A guard stood by the wall and waved a spear at Sinon. "Who goes there?"

"Sinon the Greek-hater," the old man said. "You let me in. Now let me out."

"You promised me a pig's head
if I let you in," the guard said.

"I'm off to get it now. The Greeks
left lots of food behind."

The guard nodded. He pushed
at a stone and part of the wall slid
open. Sinon patted his arm and
walked out onto the moon-
silver plain.

I ran to the gate.

"Acheron the singer!" the guard cried.

"Shush, Cottus!" I hissed. "Let me out. I'm following that man."

"Don't you go pinching any pigs' heads those Greeks left behind. The first one is mine."

"You already have a pig's head on your shoulders," I muttered and pushed through the gap in the wall.

Sinon was plodding over the plain. The Greek tents were gone, but ashes from dead fires and broken swords of dead men showed where they had been. I kept to the path around the edge of the plain and ran in the shadows of boulders.

We were close to the shore now and the moon was blocked by a huge shape. The shape of a wooden horse, almost as tall as the walls of Troy.

Sinon waved to the horse as he walked past it. At the water's edge, there was a wooden pier that the Greeks had built.

A single ship stood waiting and Sinon walked towards it. The east wind carried the voices to me:

"Is it done, Sinon?"

"It is done. They take the horse in tomorrow morning."

"That's when we will return."

A rope was untied and the ship was rowed out into the wind-chopped sea.

It was a mystery. Sinon had said they were gone for good, so why were they talking of returning?

I wandered back over the plain towards Troy and looked up at the horse. On the moonlit side, I saw something I hadn't seen on my way out to the shore.

A rope ladder hung down the side. I heard voices of men and they seemed to be coming from within. I heard the rattle of their armour and swords as they moved around.

Then I understood. And I knew what I had to do.

I sped over the silver-sanded plain and back to the walls of Troy. I called for Cottus to open the gate. "Did you see that old feller with my pig's head?" he asked as the stone swung open. "I want it on a plate."

"It'll be *your* head on a plate tomorrow if you don't let me through. Quickly! I have to warn Prince Paris!"

I ran over the cobbles till my bare feet were stinging, and up the hill till my lungs were burning. I burst into the feast and cried, "Beware of the wooden horse!"

Chapter Five

"A singerly songerly!" Paris cried
when he saw me. The wine jars were
all empty now and the royal faces
were as red as a Trojan sunrise ...
the last sunrise Troy would ever see.
Even the guards were drunk.

"The Greeks are planning a trick!"

"Singerly songerly!" Paris roared and banged the table with his knife handle.

"He wants you to give us one of your poems, Acheron," Helen cried. "Do it!"

"But..."

"Do it or we will be eating *you* in a pie at the next feast," she snarled.

I'd lost my lyre. I had no song. I had to make it up as I went along. I began:

"The Greeks they left a gift,
a wooden horse;

It isn't all it seems, you know …
of course!

The horse is stuffed with soldiers,
fully armed.

Once they're inside our walls,
they'll do us harm.

Just leave the
horse out there
upon the plain;

Or Troy will
die and never
rise again!"

Helen picked up a knife and threw it at me. I ducked and it slithered over the marble floor. "That is the worst poem I've ever heard. You should die for that!"

"But it's the truth!" I wailed.

"Acheron, you are a poet and a storyteller. It is your job to tell us *lies* – tales about how brave Paris is, when we all know that really he's a weedy little coward."

"Cowardy whobee? Songerlees
of bravebold Paris trulyful is!"
Paris tried to say.

"You, Acheron, wouldn't know the
truth if it jumped out of a pie and
smacked you in the eye. You can't go
making our feast gloomy with your
tales of Greek victory," Helen hissed.
She turned to the guards at the
table. "Execute the liar!"

I turned. I ran. I tumbled down the hill to home. I shook my mother awake and dragged her to the secret gate and out onto the windy plain.

We rested among the rocks that night and slept among the sweet scent of flowers, and the sweeter scent of freedom.

We awoke to the sound of
squealing wheels.

The wooden horse was being
dragged though the great main gates
of Troy.

Endings

You know the rest of the tale, I guess. Once inside the city, the Greek soldiers climbed out of the wooden horse and opened the gates.

The Greek army returned, just as I'd said they would.

The rest was slaughter.

Paris and every man and boy was killed – except the one boy who was hiding in the hills, watching.

Every woman and girl was carried off as a slave to Greece. Helen was taken home to her husband.

The mighty city burned and fell.
The walls cracked and crumbled in
the heat. Troy died that day.

We lived among the ruins for
many years. My mother died in time,
as mothers do.

That was a lifetime ago. There is only one Trojan left to tell the truth.

The Greek poets sing their side of the story. I am left to sing mine alone. The song is of 'The Boy Who Cried Horse'.

The trouble is I told lies. But I'm not lying now.

As Aesop the Greek storyteller said, "There is no believing a liar, even when he speaks the truth."

You believe me, don't you? I am Acheron the Liar. The last Trojan.

And that was my story.

TERRY DEARY'S
GREEK TALES

THE
TORTOISE
AND THE
DARE

OLYMPIA, GREECE, 776 BC

Ellie is furious – her twin brother Cypselis
has made a bet. If he beats Big Bacchiad in
the school Olympics foot race, their family
will receive a goat, if he loses, she will
become the bully's slave. And with the odds
stacked against him, how can she make sure
Cypselis stands a chance of winning?

Greek Tales are exciting, funny stories based
on historical events – short chapters and
illustrations throughout are perfect for
building reading confidence.

ISBN 978 0 7136 8220 5   £4.99

THE
TOWN MOUSE
AND THE
SPARTAN HOUSE

ATHENS, GREECE, 430 BC

Athens is at war with Sparta, home to
the cruellest people on Earth. But when
plague spreads through the city, Darius
is forced to leave and join his uncle,
a Spartan general. To the Spartans,
Darius is as worthless as a mouse.
How can he prove them wrong?

Greek Tales are exciting, funny stories based
on historical events – short chapters and
illustrations throughout are perfect for
building reading confidence.

ISBN 978 0 7136 8221 2   £4.99

TERRY DEARY'S
GREEK TALES
THE LION'S SLAVE

SYRACUSE, GREECE, 213 BC
Archimedes is the cleverest man in Greece.
So when the Romans attack, everyone
believes he'll find a way to save them.
Lydia, his slave, thinks so, too, and cheers
with the crowd as he creates one amazing
invention after another. But who is the
real brains behind them all?

Greek Tales are exciting, funny stories based
on historical events – short chapters and
illustrations throughout are perfect for
building reading confidence.

ISBN 978 0 7136 8222 9   £4.99